The Cautionary Tale of the
CHILDE OF HALE
by Rachel Lyon
D0347696

There once was a man called the Childe of Hale,
Who was as long as an oak tree and wide as a whale.
During the night, he'd get wet if it rained,
For his feet dangled out of the window panes.

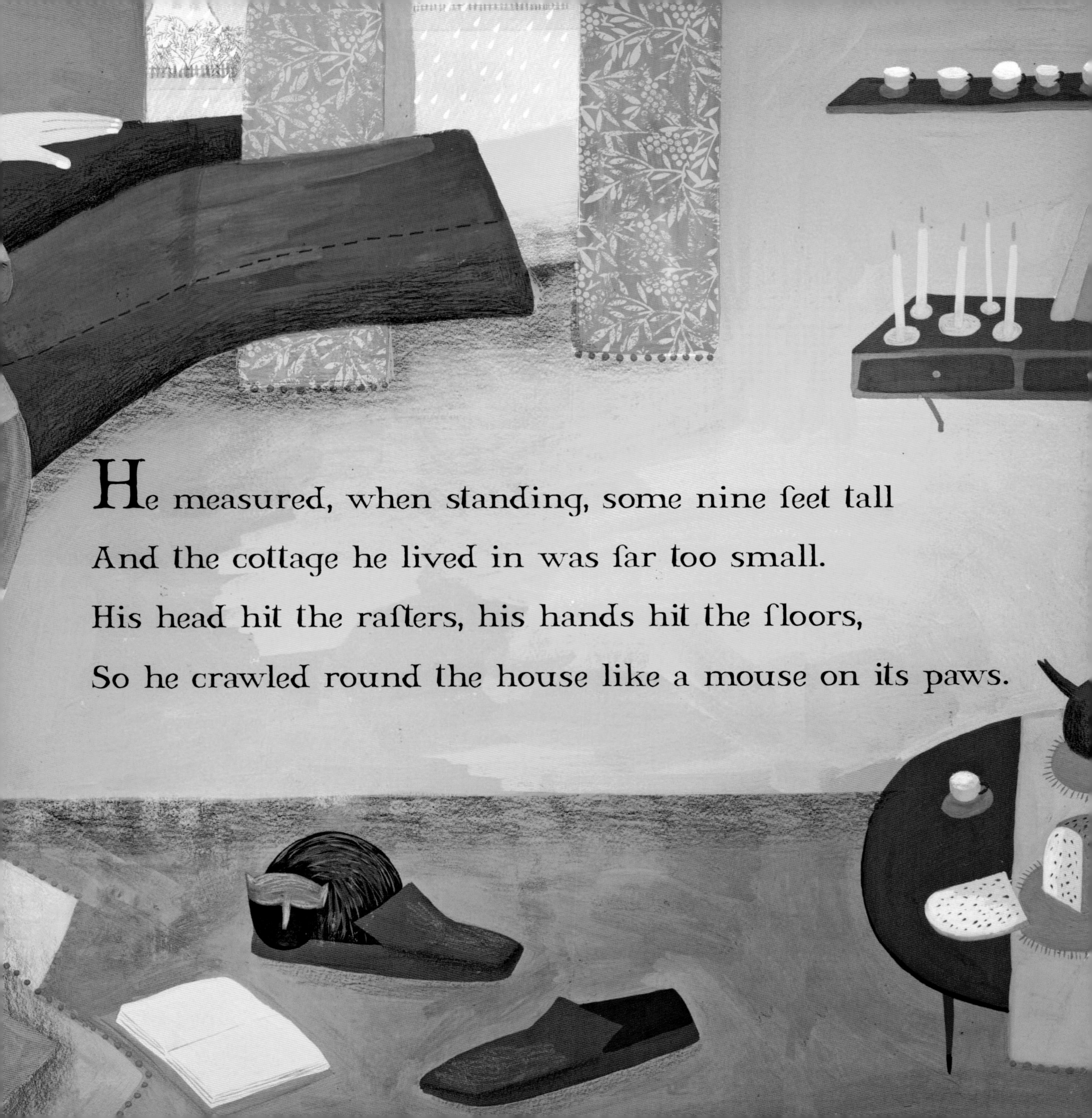

He measured, when standing, some nine feet tall
And the cottage he lived in was far too small.
His head hit the rafters, his hands hit the floors,
So he crawled round the house like a mouse on its paws.

'Til one day the Childe heard a rat-a-tat-tat.
He crawled to the window and asked, "Who is that?"
"'Tis I," said the voice of his friend from the street.
"The King is in Hale and I think you should meet."

With huffing and puffing, he squeezed out the door,
And followed his friend to a crowd by the shore.
"Ah Childe!" said the folk, as they beckoned him near
"The King is in Hale and we think you should hear,"

"Dear fellows of Hale," said the King to the crowds,
"I've heard there's a giant who touches the clouds,
And now what I tell you, to him please repeat,
For the King is in Hale and the King he must meet."

"Please sir," cried his friend, as he pushed through the crowd.
"I've already brought him," and the Childe of Hale bowed.
"My, my" said the King as he stroked at his beard
"You're a marvel of England!" And the crowd danced and cheered.

"The Queen would adore you, and the Queen you must meet.
You can stay at the Palace; I'll build you a suite.
My wishes are final - I will not relent;
You must come to London," and to London they went.

The Childe, on arrival, stood silent in awe.
His suite was so big he could fit through the door.
His chamber? Enormous! His bed? Bigger yet!
He could now sleep in comfort and never get wet!

The Queen, as her husband had promised, went wild.
She leapt in the air at the sight of the Childe.
She ordered her tailors to make him some clothes.
At last! He had trousers that reached to his toes!

The Childe had no need now to crawl like a mouse.
He didn't miss Hale or his cramped little house.
He made friends with Princes and Barons, no less!
And dined every day with the charming Princess.

'Til one day the Childe heard a rat-a-tat-tat
So he sat up in bed and he asked, "Who is that?"
"'Tis I," said the King. "Oh come quick Childe of Hale,
There's a man you must wrestle! You simply can't fail."

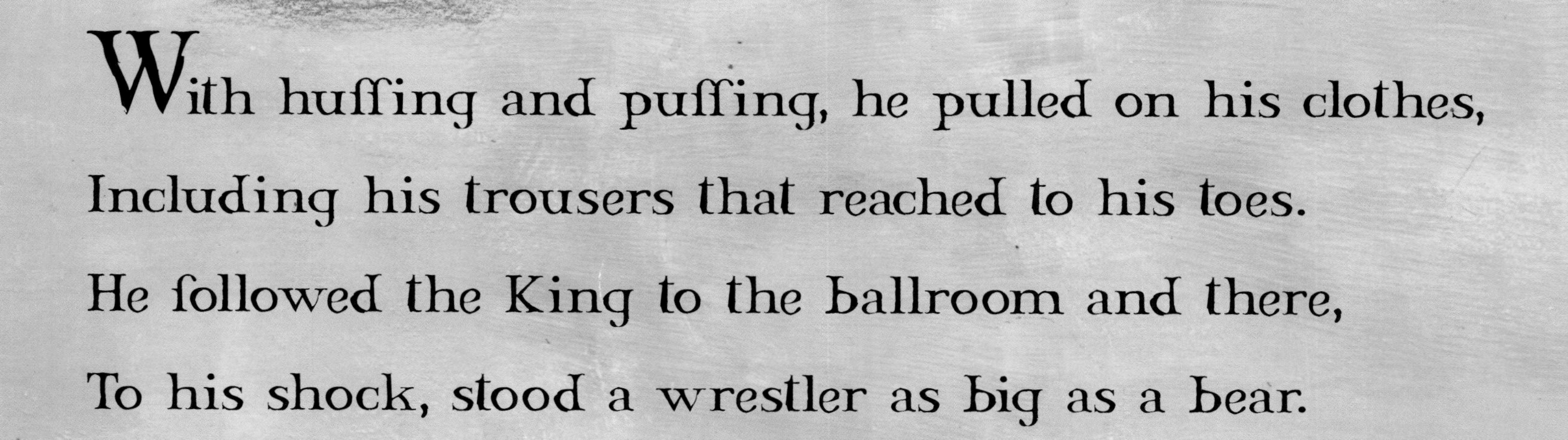

With huffing and puffing, he pulled on his clothes,
Including his trousers that reached to his toes.
He followed the King to the ballroom and there,
To his shock, stood a wrestler as big as a bear.

"The Bear," said the King, "has come here for a bout,
But you are a giant - you'll beat him, no doubt.
The prize for the winner is silver and gold,
And you are my giant, so do as you're told!"

The Princess felt sad for her good friend, the Childe:
A giant was never so gentle or mild.
She barely could watch as the Bear made a rush,
And gripped the Childe's legs and attempted to push.

But my, how amazing! Her fear was unproved,
For the Childe neither wavered, nor wobbled nor moved.
The Bear heaved and hustled, and panted and pressed,
But the Childe simply stood where he was, unimpressed.

The Bear grew exhausted. His energy spent,
He collapsed in a heap at the feet of the gent.
The King set off crying, and sobbed through the din!
"The Bear was unbeaten! I wagered he'd win!"

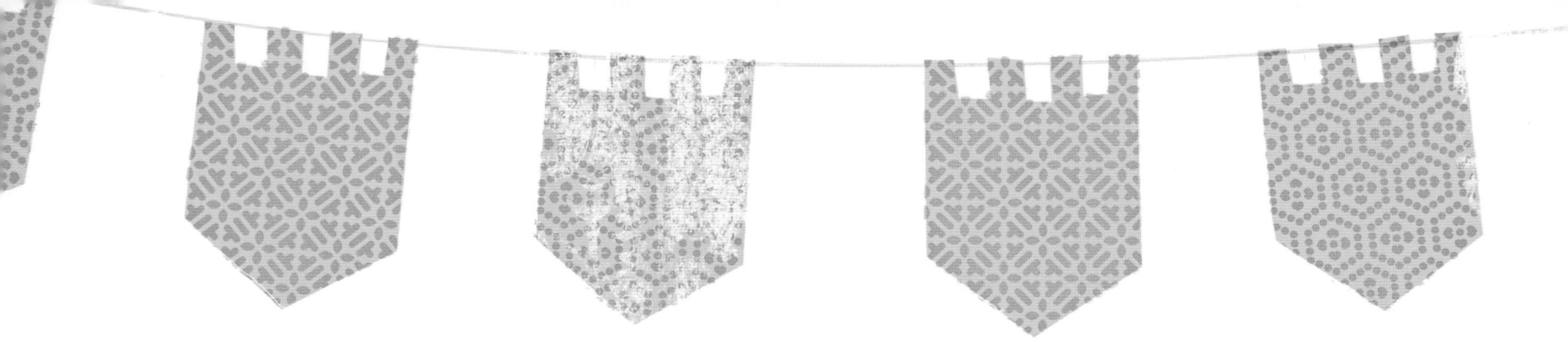

The Princess was outraged; her face grew quite pale.
"Is this why you sought him, and brought him from Hale?
To wrestle for money, pray, have you no shame?
To misuse the trust of a giant so tame?"

She fetched all the gold and she gave Childe the prize,
But nothing could dry up the tears in his eyes.
"Oh my," said the giant. "How foolish I've been,
To leave little Hale for a King and his Queen.

To leave all my friends for a bed and some clothes -
I'd rather have trousers that don't reach my toes.
Kindness, you see, is what makes us stand tall,
Whether born in a palace or a house that's too small."

There once was a man called the Childe of Hale,
Who was long as an oak tree and wide as a whale.
And if, when in Hale, you should pass by his house,
Remember the giant who lived like a mouse.

The End

The Cautionary Tale of the Childe of Hale
is inspired by the life of John Middleton
and fictionalised by author Rachel Lyon

Illustrated by Vanina Starkoff

A CIP catalogue record for this book is available at the British Library.

Maverick Arts Publishing Ltd
The Studio
Ashley House
Pulborough
RH20 1AH
+44(0) 1798 875980

PUBLISHED BY
MAVERICK ARTS PUBLISHING LTD

ISBN 978-1-84886-095-7